CLOCKWORK
OR *ALL WOUND UP*

Selected Works by Philip Pullman

Count Karlstein
How to Be Cool
Spring-Heeled Jack
The Broken Bridge
The Wonderful Story of Aladdin and the Enchanted Lamp
Clockwork or All Wound Up
The Firework-Maker's Daughter
Mossycoat
The Butterfly Tattoo
I Was a Rat! or The Scarlet Slippers
Puss in Boots: The Adventures of That Most Enterprising Feline
The Scarecrow and his Servant
The Adventures of the New Cut Gang
The Good Man Jesus and the Scoundrel Christ
Grimm Tales: For Young and Old

HIS DARK MATERIALS TRILOGY
Northern Lights
The Subtle Knife
The Amber Spyglass

HIS DARK MATERIALS COMPANION BOOKS
Lyra's Oxford
Once Upon a Time in the North

THE BOOK OF DUST TRILOGY
La Belle Sauvage

THE SALLY LOCKHART QUARTET
The Ruby in the Smoke
The Shadow in the North
The Tiger in the Well
The Tin Princess

GRAPHIC NOVELS
The Adventures of John Blake

PHILIP PULLMAN

CLOCKWORK
OR *ALL WOUND UP*

Illustrated by Peter Bailey

PUFFIN

PUFFIN BOOKS

UK | USA | Canada | Ireland | Australia
India | New Zealand | South Africa

Puffin Books is part of the Penguin Random House group of companies
whose addresses can be found at global.penguinrandomhouse.com.

www.penguin.co.uk
www.puffin.co.uk
www.ladybird.co.uk

Penguin
Random House
UK

First published by Doubleday 1996
Published by Corgi Yearling edition 1997, 2004
Published in this edition 2018

001

Set in 12.5/20.5 pt Minister Std Light
Typeset by Jouve (UK), Milton Keynes
Printed in Great Britain by Clays Ltd, St Ives plc

A CIP catalogue record for this book is available from the British Library

ISBN: 978–0–241–32631–2

All correspondence to:
Puffin Books
Penguin Random House Children's
80 Strand, London WC2R 0RL

CONTENTS

CLOCKWORK: A PREFACE

IN THE old days, when this story took place, time used to run by clockwork. Real clockwork, I mean, springs and cogwheels and gears and pendulums and so on. When you took it apart you could see how it worked, and how to put it together again. Nowadays, time runs by electricity and vibrating crystals of quartz and goodness knows what else. You can even buy a watch that's powered by a solar panel, and sets itself several times a day by picking up a radio signal, and never runs a second late. Clocks and watches like that might as well work by witchcraft for all the sense I can make of them.

Real clockwork is quite mysterious enough. Take a spring, for instance, like the mainspring of an alarm clock. It's made of tempered steel, with an edge that's sharp enough to draw blood. If you play about with it carelessly it'll spring up and strike at you like a snake, and put out your eye. Or take a weight, the kind of iron weight that drives the mighty clocks they have in church towers. If your head were under that weight, and if the weight fell, it would dash out your brains on the floor.

But with the help of a few gears and pins, and a little balance wheel oscillating to and fro, or a pendulum swinging from side to side, the strength of the spring and the power of the weight are led harmlessly through the clock to drive the hands.

And once you've wound up a clock, there's something frightful in the way it keeps on going at its own relentless pace. Its hands move steadily round the dial as if they had a mind of their own. Tick, tock, tick, tock! Bit by bit they move, and tick us steadily on towards the grave.

Some stories are like that. Once you've wound them up, nothing will stop them; they move on forwards till they reach their destined end, and no matter how much the characters would like to change their fate, they can't. This is one of those stories. And now it's all wound up, we can begin.

PART ONE

ONCE UPON a time (when time ran by clockwork), a strange event took place in a little German town. Actually, it was a series of events, all fitting together like the parts of a clock, and although each person saw a different part, no-one saw the whole of it; but here it is, as well as I can tell it.

It began on a winter's evening, when the townsfolk were gathering in the White Horse Tavern. The snow was blowing down from the mountains, and the wind was making the bells

5

shift restlessly in the church tower. The windows were steamed up, the stove was blazing brightly, Putzi the old black cat was snoozing on the hearth; and the air was full of the rich smells of sausage and sauerkraut, of tobacco and beer. Gretl the little barmaid, the landlord's daughter, was hurrying to and fro with foaming mugs and steaming plates.

The door opened, and fat white flakes of snow swirled in, to faint away into water as they met the heat of the parlour. The incomers, Herr Ringelmann the clockmaker and his apprentice Karl, stamped their boots and shook the snow off their greatcoats.

'It's Herr Ringelmann!' said the Burgomaster. 'Well, old friend, come and drink some beer with me! And a mug for young what's his name, your apprentice.'

Karl the apprentice nodded his thanks and went to sit by himself in a corner. His expression was dark and gloomy.

'What's the matter with young thingamajig?' said the Burgomaster. 'He looks as if he's swallowed a thundercloud.'

'Oh, I shouldn't worry,' said the old clockmaker, sitting down at the table with his friends. 'He's anxious about tomorrow. His apprenticeship is coming to an end, you see.'

'Ah, of course!' said the Burgomaster. It was the custom that when a clockmaker's apprentice finished his period of service, he made a new figure for the great clock of Glockenheim. 'So we're to have a new piece of clockwork in the tower! Well, I look forward to seeing it tomorrow.'

'I remember when my apprenticeship came to an end,' said Herr Ringelmann. 'I couldn't sleep for thinking about what would happen when my figure came out of the clock. Supposing I hadn't counted the cogs properly? Supposing the spring was too stiff? Supposing – oh, a thousand things go through your mind. It's a heavy responsibility.'

'Maybe so, but I've never seen the lad look so gloomy before,' said someone else. 'And he's not a cheerful fellow at the best of times.'

And it seemed to the other drinkers that Herr Ringelmann himself was a little down-hearted, but he raised his mug with the rest of them and changed the conversation to another topic.

'I hear young Fritz the novelist is going to read us his new story tonight,' he said.

'So I believe,' said the Burgomaster. 'I hope it's not as terrifying as the last one he read to us. D'you know, I woke three times that night and found my hair on end, just thinking about it!'

'I don't know if it's more frightening hearing them here in the parlour, or reading them later on your own,' said someone else.

'It's worse on your own, believe me,' said another. 'You can feel the ghostly fingers creeping up your spine, and even when you know what's going to happen next you can't help jumping when it does.'

The great clock of Glockenheim was the most amazing piece of machinery in the whole of Germany. If you wanted to see all the figures you would have to watch it for a whole year, because the mechanism was so complex that it took twelve months to complete its movement. There were all the saints, each coming out on their own day; there was Death, with his scythe and hourglass; there were over a hundred figures altogether. Herr Ringelmann was in charge of it all. There never was a clock like it, I promise.

Then they argued about whether it was more terrifying to hear a ghost story when you didn't know what was going to happen (because it took you by surprise) or when you did (because there was the suspense of waiting for it). They all enjoyed ghost stories, and Fritz's in particular, for he was a talented storyteller.

The subject of their conversation, Fritz the writer himself, was a cheerful-looking young man who had been eating his supper at the other end of the parlour. He joked with the landlord, he laughed with his neighbours, and when he'd finished, he called for another mug of beer, gathered up the untidy pile of manuscript beside his plate, and went to talk to Karl.

'Hello, old boy,' he said cheerfully. 'All set for tomorrow? I'm looking forward to it! What are you going to show us?'

Karl scowled and turned away.

'The artistic temperament,' said the landlord wisely. 'Drink up your beer, and have another on

The artistic temperament! What nonsense! There's no such thing. Only amateurs have temperaments. Real artists get on with the job and don't fuss about it. If you hear anyone talking about the artistic temperament, you can be sure they don't know what they're talking about.

the house, in honour of tomorrow.'

'Put poison in, and I'll drink it then,' muttered Karl.

'What?' said Fritz, who could hardly believe his ears. The two of them were sitting right at the end of the bar, and Fritz moved so as to turn his back on the rest of the company and speak to Karl in private. 'What's the matter, old fellow?' he went on quietly. 'You've been working at your masterpiece for months! Surely you're not worried about it? It can't fail!'

Karl looked at him with a face full of savage bitterness.

'I haven't made a figure,' he muttered. 'I couldn't do it. I've failed, Fritz. The clock will chime tomorrow, and everyone will be looking up to see what I've done, and nothing will come out, nothing . . .' He groaned softly, and turned away. 'I can't face them!' he went on. 'I should go and throw myself off the tower now and have done with it!'

'Oh, come on, don't talk like that!' said Fritz, who had never seen his friend so bitter. 'You must have a word with old Herr Ringelmann – ask his advice – tell him you've hit a snag – he's a decent old fellow, he'll help you out!'

'You don't understand,' said Karl passionately. 'Everything's so easy for you! You just sit at your desk and put pen to paper, and stories come pouring out! You don't know what it is to sweat and strain for hours on end with no ideas at all, or to struggle with materials that break, and tools that go blunt, or to tear your hair out trying to find a new variation on the same old theme – I tell you, Fritz, it's a wonder I haven't blown my brains out long before this! Well, it won't be long now. Tomorrow morning you can all laugh at me. Karl, the failure. Karl, the hopeless. Karl, the first apprentice to fail in hundreds of years of clockmaking. I don't care. I shall be lying at the bottom of the river, under the ice.'

Fritz had had to stop himself interrupting when Karl spoke about the difficulty of working. Stories are just as hard as clocks to put together, and they can go wrong just as easily – as we shall see with Fritz's own story in a page or two. Still, Fritz was an optimist, and Karl was a pessimist, and that makes all the difference in the world.

Putzi the cat, waking from his snooze on the hearth, came and rubbed his back against Karl's legs. Karl kicked him savagely away.

'Steady on,' said Fritz.

But Karl only scowled. He drank deeply and wiped his mouth with the back of his hand before banging the mug on the counter and calling for more. Gretl the young barmaid looked anxiously at Fritz, because she was only a child, and wasn't sure whether she should be serving someone in Karl's condition.

'Give him some more,' said Fritz. 'He's not drunk, poor fellow, he's unhappy. I'll keep an eye on him, don't you worry.'

So Gretl poured some more beer for Karl, and the clockmaker's apprentice scowled and turned away. Fritz was worried about him, but he couldn't stay there any longer, because the patrons were calling for him.

'Come on, Fritz! Where's that story?'

'Sing for your supper! Come on! We're all waiting!' 'What's it about this time, eh? Skeletons, or ghosts?'

'I hope it's a nice bloody murder!'

'No, I hear he's got something quite different for us this time. Something quite new.'

'I've got a feeling it's going to be more horrible than anything we could imagine,' said old Johann the woodcutter.

While the drinkers ordered more mugs of beer to see them through the story, and filled their pipes and settled themselves comfortably, Fritz gathered up his manuscript and took up his place by the stove.

To tell the truth, Fritz was less comfortable himself than he had ever been before at one of these storytelling evenings, because of what Karl had just told him, and because of the theme of his story – of the start of it, anyway. But after all, it wasn't about Karl. The subject was really quite different.

(There was another private reason for Fritz to be nervous. The fact was, he hadn't actually finished the story. He'd written the start all right, and it was terrific, but he hadn't been able to think of an ending. He was just going to wind up the story, set it going, and make up the end when he got there. As I said just now, he was an optimist.)

'We're all ready and waiting,' said the Burgo-master. 'I'm looking forward to this story, even if it does make my hair stand on end. What's it called?'

'It's called –' said Fritz, with a nervous glance at Karl – 'it's called "Clockwork".'

'Ah! Very appropriate!' cried old Herr Ringelmann. 'Did you hear that, Karl? This is a story in your honour, my boy!'

Karl scowled and looked down at the floor.

'No, no,' said Fritz hastily, 'this story isn't about Karl, or the clock in our town, no, not at all. It's quite different. It just happens to be called "Clockwork".'

'Well, set it going,' said someone. 'We're all ready.'

So Fritz cleared his throat and arranged his papers and began to read:

Fritz's Story

'I wonder if any of you remember the extraordinary business at the palace a few years ago? They tried to hush it up, but some details came out, and a bizarre mystery it was, too. It seems that Prince Otto had taken his young son Florian hunting, together with an old friend of the royal family, Baron Stelgratz. It was the dead of winter – just like now. They'd set off in a sledge for the hunting lodge up in the mountains, well wrapped up against the cold, and they weren't expected back for a week or so.

'Well, what should happen but that only two nights later, the sentry on duty at the palace gate saw a commotion down the road, and heard the whinnying of horses – whinnying in panic – making a terrible racket; and it looked, though he couldn't be sure, as if a sledge was being driven towards the palace by a madman.

'The sentry raised the alarm, and called for lights, and when the sledge got close enough, they could see that it was the royal sledge, the very one the prince had set off in only two nights before. It was hurtling up the road behind those terrified horses, and it wasn't going to stop; and the sergeant of the guard gave orders to drag the palace gates open quickly before it crashed.

'They got them open just in time. The sledge rushed through, and then drove round and round the courtyard, for the horses were mad with fear and couldn't stop. The poor beasts were covered with foam and their eyes were rolling, and the sledge would be going round that courtyard still if one of the runners hadn't caught on a mounting block and turned the whole thing over.

'Out fell the driver, and out fell a bundle from the back of the sledge. A servant hastened to pick it up, and found little Prince Florian wrapped in a fur rug, safe and warm and half asleep.

'But as for the driver . . .

'Well, as soon as the sentries came close, they saw who it was. It was none other than Prince Otto himself, stark dead, as cold as ice, with his eyes wide and staring ahead of him, his left hand gripping the reins so tight they had to be cut loose, and (this was the strangest part) his right hand still moving, lashing the whip up and down, up and down, up and down.

'They covered him up so the princess wouldn't see him, and took little Prince Florian to her to prove he was alive and well, because he was their only child.

'But what was to be done with Prince Otto? They took his body into the palace and sent for the Royal Physician, a worthy old man who'd studied in Heidelberg and Paris and Bologna, and who'd published a treatise on the location of the soul; he'd studied geology, and hydrology, and physiology, but he'd never seen anything like this before. A dead body that wouldn't keep still! Imagine that! Stretched out icy-cold on a marble slab, with its right arm lashing and lashing and lashing with no sign that it was ever going to stop.

'The physician locked the door to keep the servants out, and brought the lamp closer, and bent low to look, and then his eye was caught by

There was a lot of argument about the location of the soul in those days. Some philosophers thought it was located in the brain, some in the heart, some in the pineal gland, whatever that is. They even used to weigh people before and after they died, to see whether they weighed less when the soul had left them. I don't know whether they did or not.

something in the clumsy arrangement of the clothes. So, avoiding that lashing right arm, he carefully unfastened the cloak and the fur coat and the under-jacket and the shirt, and laid the prince's chest bare.

'And there it was: a gash across his breast just over the heart, crudely sewn up with a dozen stitches. The physician got his scissors and snipped them away, and then he nearly fainted with surprise, because when he opened the wound, there was no heart there. Instead, there was a little piece of clockwork: just a few cogs and springs and a balance wheel, attached in subtle ways to the prince's veins and tick-tick-

ticking away merrily, in perfect time with the lashing of his arm.

'Well, you can imagine how the physician crossed himself and took a sip of brandy to calm his nerves. Who wouldn't? Then he carefully cut the attachments and lifted out the clockwork, and as he did so, the arm fell still, just like that.'

As he got to that point in his story, Fritz paused for a sip of beer, and to see how his audience was taking it. The silence in the inn was profound. Every single customer was sitting so still they might have been dead themselves, except for their wide eyes and expressions of tense excitement. He had never had such a success!

He turned the page and read on:

Fritz's Story (continued)

'Well, the physician sewed up Prince Otto's wound, and let it be known that the prince had died of apoplexy. The servants who'd carried the body in thought differently; they knew a dead man when they saw one, even if his arm was moving; at any rate, the official version was that Prince Otto had suffered a contusion of the brain, and that his love for his son had kept him alive just long enough to drive him safely home. He was buried with a good deal of ceremony, and everyone was in mourning for six months.

'As for what had happened to Baron Stelgratz, the other member of the hunting party, no-one could guess. The whole affair was shrouded in mystery.

'But the Royal Physician had an idea. There was one man who might be able to explain what had happened, and that was the great Dr Kalmenius of Schatzberg, of whom very few people had heard; but those who did know of him said he was the cleverest man in Europe. For making clockwork, he had no equal, not even our good Herr Ringelmann. He could make intricate pieces of calculating apparatus that worked out the positions of all the stars and the planets, and answer any mathematical question.

'Dr Kalmenius could have made his fortune if he'd wanted to, but he wasn't interested in fortune or in fame. He was interested in something far deeper than that. He would spend hours sitting in graveyards, contemplating the mysteries of life and death. Some said he experimented on dead bodies. Others said he was in league with the powers of darkness. No-one knew for certain. But one thing they did know was that he used to walk about at night, pulling behind him a little sledge containing what-ever secret matter he was working on at the time.

'What did he look like, this philosopher of the night? He was very tall and thin, with a prominent nose and jaw. His eyes blazed like coals in caverns of darkness. His hair was long and grey, and he wore a black cloak with a loose hood like that of a monk; he had a harsh grating voice, and his expression was full of savage curiosity.

There was something uncanny about Dr Kalmenius's clockwork. He made little figures that sang and spoke and played chess, and shot tiny arrows from tiny bows, and played the harpsichord as well as Mozart. You can see some of his clockwork figures today in the museum at Schatzberg, but they don't work any more. It's odd, because all the parts are in place, and in perfect order, and they should work; but they don't. It's almost as if they had . . . died.

'And that was the man who—'

Fritz stopped.

He swallowed, and his eyes moved to the door. Everyone followed his gaze. The parlour had never been so still. No-one moved, no-one dared to breathe, for the latch was lifting.

The door slowly opened.

On the threshold stood a man in a long black cloak with a loose hood like a monk's. His grey hair hung down on either side of his face: a long, narrow face with a prominent nose and jaw, and eyes that looked like burning coals in caverns of darkness.

Oh, the silence as he stepped inside! Every single person in the parlour was gaping, mouth open, eyes wide; and when they saw what the stranger was pulling behind him – a little sledge with something wrapped in canvas – more than one crossed themselves and stood up in fear.

The stranger bowed.

'Dr Kalmenius of Schatzberg, at your service,' he said, in a harsh, grating voice. 'I have come a long way tonight, and I am cold. A glass of brandy!'

The landlord poured it hastily. The stranger drained it at once and held out the glass for more. Still nobody moved.

'So silent?' said Dr Kalmenius, looking around mockingly. 'One might think one had arrived among the dead!'

The Burgomaster swallowed hard and got to his feet.

'I beg your pardon, Dr – er – Kalmenius, but the fact is that—'

And he looked at Fritz, who was staring at Dr Kalmenius with horror. The young man was as pale as the paper in his hand. His eyes were nearly starting from his head, his hair was standing on end, and a ghastly sweat had broken out on his forehead.

'Yes, my good sir?' said Dr Kalmenius.

'I – I—' said Fritz, and swallowed convulsively.

The Burgomaster intervened: 'The fact is that our young friend is a writer of stories, Doctor, and he was reading us one of his tales when you arrived.'

'Ah! How delightful!' said Dr Kalmenius. 'I should greatly enjoy hearing the rest of your story, young sir. Please don't feel inhibited by my presence – carry on as if I weren't here at all.'

A little cry broke from Fritz's throat. With a sudden movement he crumpled all his sheets of paper together and thrust them into the stove, where they blazed up high.

'I beg you,' he cried, 'have nothing to do with this man!'

And like someone who has seen the Devil, he ran out of the inn as fast as he could.

Dr Kalmenius broke into a wild and mocking laugh, and at that, several other good citizens followed Fritz's example, and left their pipes and their mugs of beer, grabbed their coats and hats, and were off, not even daring to look the stranger in the eye.

Herr Ringelmann and the Burgomaster were almost the last to leave. The old clockmaker thought he should say something to a fellow craftsman, but his tongue was mute, and the Burgomaster thought he should either welcome the eminent Dr Kalmenius or send him on his way, but his nerve failed; and the two old men took their sticks and hurried away as fast as they could.

Little Gretl was clinging to her father the landlord, watching it all with wide eyes.

'Well!' said Dr Kalmenius. 'You keep early hours in this town. I will take another glass of brandy.'

The landlord poured with a shaking hand, and ushered Gretl out, for this was no company for a child.

Dr Kalmenius drained the brandy at once, and called for yet another.

'And perhaps this gentleman will join me,' he said, turning to the corner of the bar.

For there sat Karl still. In the rush of all the other customers to leave, he had not moved. He turned his glowering face, now flushed with drink and sullen with self-hatred, to glare at the stranger, but he could not meet those mocking eyes, and he dropped his gaze to the floor.

'Bring a glass for my companion,' said Dr Kalmenius to the landlord, 'and then you may leave us.'

The landlord put the bottle and another glass on the bar, and fled. Only five minutes before, the parlour had been full to bursting; but now Dr Kalmenius and Karl were alone, and the inn was so quiet that Karl could hear the whisper of flames in the stove, and the ticking of the old clock in the corner, even over the beating of his own heart.

Dr Kalmenius poured some brandy, and pushed the glass along the bar. Karl said nothing.

He bore the stranger's stare for nearly a minute, and then he banged his fist on the counter and cried:

'God damn you, what do you want?'

'Of you, sir? I want nothing from you.'

'You came here on purpose to jeer at me!'

'To jeer at you? Come, come, we have better clowns than you in Schatzberg. Should I come all this way to laugh at a young man whose face shows nothing but unhappiness? Come, drink up! Look cheerful! It is your morning of triumph tomorrow!'

Karl groaned and turned away, but Dr Kalmenius's mocking voice continued:

'Yes, the unveiling of a new figure for the famous clock of Glockenheim is an important occasion. Do you know, I tried to find a bed in five different inns before I came here, and they were all full up. Visitors from all over Germany – gentlemen and ladies – craftsmen, clockmakers, experts in all kinds of machinery – all come to see your new figure, your masterpiece! Isn't that something to be joyful about? Drink, my friend, drink!'

Karl snatched the glass and swallowed the fiery liquor.

'There won't be a new figure,' he muttered.

'What's this?'

'I said there won't be a new figure. I haven't made one. I couldn't. I wasted all my time, and when it was too late I found I couldn't do it. There you are. Now you can laugh at me. Go on.'

'Oh, dear, dear,' said Dr Kalmenius solemnly. 'Laugh? I wouldn't dream of it. I've come here to help you.'

'What? You? How?'

Dr Kalmenius smiled. It was like a flame suddenly breaking out of an ash-covered log, and Karl recoiled. The old man came closer.

'You see,' he said, 'I think you may have overlooked the philosophical implications of our craft. You know how to regulate a watch and repair a church clock, but had you ever considered that our lives are clockwork, too?'

'I don't understand,' said Karl.

'We can control the future, my boy, just as we wind up the mechanism in a clock. Say to yourself: I *will* win that race – I *will* come first – and you wind up the future like clockwork. The world has no choice but to obey! Can the hands of that old clock in the corner decide to stop? Can the spring in your watch decide to wind itself up and run backwards? No! They have no choice. And nor has the future, once you have wound it up.'

Now we're getting to the heart of it. This is Dr Kalmenius's philosophy. This is what he wants Karl to believe. Well, there may be something in it. There are plenty of people who think they only have to wish for something, and it'll come true. Doesn't everyone think like that when they buy a lottery ticket? And there's no doubt, it's a pleasant thing to imagine. But there's a flaw in it . . .

. . . and here it is: you don't win races by wishing, you win them by running faster than everyone else. And to do that you have to train hard and strive your utmost, and sometimes even that isn't enough, because another runner just might be more talented than you are. Here's the truth: if you want something, you <u>can</u> have it, but only if you want everything that goes with it, including all the hard work and the despair, and only if you're willing to risk failure. That's the problem with Karl: he was afraid of failing, so he never really tried.

'Impossible,' said Karl, who was feeling more and more light-headed.

'Oh, but it's easy! What would you like? Wealth? A beautiful bride? Wind up the future, my friend! Say what you want, and it will be yours! Fame, power, riches – what would you like?'

'You know very well what I want!' cried Karl. 'I want a figure for the clock! Something to show for all the time I should have spent in making it! Anything to avoid the shame I'll feel tomorrow!'

'Nothing could be easier,' said Dr Kalmenius. 'You spoke – and there is what you wished for.'

And he pointed to the little sledge he'd pulled behind him into the parlour. The runners stood in a puddle of melted snow, and the canvas cover was damp.

'What is it?' said Karl, who had suddenly become very afraid.

'Uncover it! Take off the canvas!'

Karl got unsteadily to his feet and slowly untied the rope holding the cover down. Then he pulled the canvas off.

In the sledge was the most perfect piece of metal sculpture he had ever seen. It was the figure of a knight in armour, made of gleaming silvery metal, holding a sharp sword. Karl gasped at the detail, and walked round looking at it from all angles. Every piece of armour-plating was riveted in such a way that it would move smoothly over the one below, and as for the sword—

He touched it, and drew his hand back at once, looking at the blood running down his fingers.

'It's like a razor,' he said.

'Only the best will do for Sir Ironsoul,' said Dr Kalmenius.

'Sir Ironsoul . . . What a piece of work! Oh, if this were in the tower among the other figures, my name would be made for ever!' said Karl bitterly. 'And how does he move? What does he do? He does work by clockwork, I suppose? Or is there some kind of goblin in there? A spirit or a devil of some kind?'

With a smooth whirr and a ticking of delicate machinery, the figure began to move. The knight raised his sword and turned his helmeted head to look for Karl, and then stepped off the sledge and moved towards him.

'No! What's he doing?' said Karl in alarm, backing away.

Sir Ironsoul kept going. Karl moved aside, but the figure turned too, and before Karl could

35

dodge away, he was pinned in the corner, with the little knight's sword moving closer and closer.

'What's he doing? That sword is sharp – stop it, Doctor! Make it stop!'

Dr Kalmenius whistled three or four bars of a simple, haunting little tune, and Sir Ironsoul fell still. The point of the sword was right at Karl's throat.

The apprentice eased his way past the figure and sank onto a chair, weak with fear.

'What – who – how did it start? This is uncanny! Did you set it off?'

'Oh, I didn't start him,' said Dr Kalmenius. 'You did.'

'I did? How?'

'It was something you said. His mechanism is so delicate, so perfectly balanced, that one word and one word alone will start him moving. And he's such a clever little fellow! Once he's heard that word, he won't rest until his sword is in the throat that uttered it.'

'What word?' said Karl fearfully. 'What did I say? Clockwork . . . goblin . . . move . . . work . . . spirit . . . devil . . .'

Once again Sir Ironsoul began to move. He turned round implacably, found Karl, and set off towards him. The apprentice was out of his chair in a flash and cowering in the corner.

'That was it!' he cried. 'Stop it again, please, Doctor!'

Dr Kalmenius whistled once more, and the figure stopped.

'What is that tune?' said Karl. 'Why does he stop for that?'

'It's a little tune called "The Flowers of Lapland",' said Dr Kalmenius. 'He likes that, bless him. He stands still to listen to it, and that tips his balance wheel the other way, and then he stops. What a marvel! What a piece of work!'

'I'm afraid of him.'

'Oh, come, come! Afraid of a little tin man who likes a pretty tune?'

'It's uncanny. It's not like a machine at all. I don't like it.'

'Well, that's a great shame. What will you do without him tomorrow? I shall be watching with great interest.'

'No, no!' said Karl, in anguish. 'I didn't mean . . . Oh, I don't know what I mean!'

'Do you want him?'

'Yes. No!' cried Karl, beating his fists together. 'I don't know. Yes!'

'Then he is yours,' said Dr Kalmenius. 'You have wound up the future, my boy! It has already begun to tick!'

And before Karl could change his mind, the clockwork-maker gathered his long cloak around him, swept the hood up over his head, and vanished out of the door with his sledge.

Karl ran to the door after him, but the snow was so thick that he could see nothing. Dr Kalmenius had vanished.

Karl turned back into the parlour and sat down weakly. The little figure stood perfectly still, with its sword upraised, and its blank metal face gazing at the young apprentice.

'He wasn't a man,' Karl muttered. 'No man could make this. He was an evil spirit! He was the dev—'

He clapped his hands over his mouth and looked in terror at Sir Ironsoul, who stood motionless.

'I nearly said it!' Karl whispered to himself. 'I mustn't ever forget – and the tune! How does it go? If I can remember that, I'll be safe . . .'

He tried to whistle it, but his mouth was too dry; he tried to hum it, but his voice was shaking. He held out his hands and looked at them. They were trembling like dry leaves.

'Perhaps if I have another drink . . .' he said.

He poured some more brandy, splashing most of it on the counter before he got some in the glass. He swallowed it quickly.

'That's better . . . Well, after all, I *could* put him in the clock. And if I bolted him to the frame, he'd be safe enough. He wouldn't be able to get out of that, no matter what words anyone said . . .'

He looked around him fearfully. The parlour was as silent as the grave. Then he lifted the curtain and peered through the window, but there was not a single light in the town square. Everyone in the world seemed to have gone to bed, and the only beings awake were the clockmaker's apprentice and the little silvery figure with the sword.

'Yes, I'll do it!' he said.

So he threw the canvas over Sir Ironsoul, hastily pulled on his coat and hat, and hurried out to unlock the tower and prepare the clock.

Now, as it happened, there was one other person awake, and that was Gretl, the landlord's little daughter. She couldn't sleep at all, and the reason for that was Fritz's story. There was one thing she couldn't get out of her mind. It wasn't the clockwork in the dead prince's breast; it wasn't the horses foaming with terror or the dead driver behind them; it was the young Prince Florian.

She thought: poor little boy, to travel home in that frightful way! She tried to imagine what terrors he must have faced, alone in the sledge with his dead father, and she shivered under her blankets, and wished that she could comfort him.

And because she couldn't sleep, she thought she'd go down and sit by the stove in the parlour for a while, because her bed was cold. So she wrapped a blanket around her shoulders and tiptoed down the stairs just as the great clock in the tower was chiming midnight. There was no-

Gretl was kind-hearted, you see. Her heart was in the right place. Her heart was warm, her heart was tender, she had a heart of gold. You know those expressions? There are some people, like Gretl, who can't hear of anyone else's problems without suffering almost as much as they do. The world is a cruel place sometimes, and warm-hearted people do most of the good in it. And much of the time, they're mocked and scorned for their pains.

one in the parlour, of course, and the lamp was burning low, so she didn't notice the little canvas-covered figure in the corner, and sat down to warm her hands at the stove.

'What a strange story that was going to be!' she said to herself. 'I'm not sure that people ought to tell stories like that. I don't mind ghosts and skeletons, but I think Fritz went too far that time. And didn't everyone jump when the old man came in! It was as if Fritz conjured him up out of nothing. Like Dr Faust, conjuring up the devil . . .'

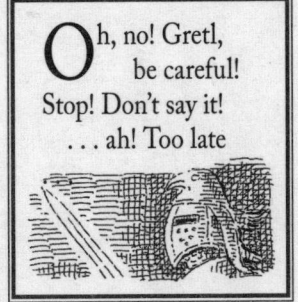

Oh, no! Gretl, be careful! Stop! Don't say it! . . . ah! Too late

And the sheet of canvas fell softly to the floor, and the little metal figure turned his head, and raised his sword, and began to move towards her.

PART TWO

WHEN PRINCE Otto married his Princess Mariposa, the whole city rejoiced: fireworks were lit in the public gardens, bands played all night in the ballrooms, and flags and banners waved from every rooftop.

'At last we'll have an heir!' the people said, for they had been afraid that the dynasty would come to an end.

But time went by, and more time, and no child came to Prince Otto and Princess Mariposa. They

The princess was called Mariposa. She was very beautiful, but what princess isn't? Being beautiful is their profession. Princess Mariposa spent most of her time shopping. The dress designers let her buy dresses at half-price, because she wore them at fashionable parties and made the designers famous. If you want to buy things cheap, it helps to be rich, strange as it seems. Poor people always have to pay the full price.

sought the opinions of the finest doctors, but still no child came. They made a pilgrimage to Rome to seek the blessing of the Holy Father, but still no child came. Finally, as Princess Mariposa stood at the palace window, she heard the chiming of the cathedral clock, and said, 'I wish I had a child as sound as a bell and as true as a clock'; and when she had said those words, she felt her heart lift.

And before the year was out, she did have a child. But alas for her and for everyone, her labour was hard and painful, and when the baby had taken one breath in this world, he could take no more, and he died in the arms of the nurse. Princess Mariposa knew nothing of that, for she was in a dreadful swoon, and no-one could say whether she would live or die. As for Prince Otto, he was nearly out of his mind with fury. He snatched the dead child from the nurse's arms and said, 'I will have an heir, come what may!'

He ran down to the stables and ordered the grooms to saddle his fastest horse, and with the dead child clasped to his breast he galloped away.

Where was he going? North, and further north, until he came to the workshop of Dr Kalmenius, near the silver mines of Schatzberg.

There it was that the great clockwork-maker created his wonders, from the celestial clocks that told the position of every planet for the next twenty-five thousand years to the little figures that danced, and rode miniature ponies, and shot tiny arrows, and played the harpsichord.

'Well?' said Dr Kalmenius.

Prince Otto stood in his riding-cloak with the snow still white on his shoulders, and held out the body of his child.

'Make me another child!' he said. 'My son is dead, and his mother lies between life and death! Dr Kalmenius, I command you to make me a child of clockwork who will not die!'

Even Prince Otto, in his madness, didn't believe that a clockwork toy could resemble a living child;

but the silver they mined in Schatzberg was not the same as other metals. It was malleable and soft and lustrous, with a bloom on it like that on a butterfly's wing. And as for the great clockwork-maker, the task was a challenge to his artistry that he couldn't resist, and so, while Prince Otto buried the dead child, Dr Kalmenius set to work to make the new one. He smelted the ore and refined the silver, and beat it into a subtle thinness; he spun gold into filaments finer than spiders' silk, and attached each one separately to the little head; he cast and filed and tempered, he soldered and riveted and bolted, he timed and adjusted and regulated, until the little mainspring was tight, and the little escapement on its jewelled bearings was ticking back and forth with perfect accuracy.

When the clockwork child was ready, Dr Kalmenius gave him to Prince Otto, who scrutinized him carefully. The baby was breathing and moving and smiling and even, by some secret art, warm. In every way he looked exactly like the child who had died. Prince Otto wrapped his cloak around the baby, and rode back to the palace, where he laid the child in the arms of Princess Mariposa; and the princess opened her eyes, and the joy of seeing her own child, as she thought, alive and well, brought her back from the brink of the grave. And besides, she looked so pretty with a child in her arms; she had always known she would.

They named him Florian. A year went by, two years, three, and the little boy grew up beloved by everyone, happy and sturdy and clever. Prince Otto took him riding on a little pony, taught him to shoot a bow and arrow; he danced, he picked out tunes on the harpsichord; he grew stronger and bigger, more merry and lively all the time.

But in the fifth year of his life, the little prince began to show signs of a disturbing illness. There was a painful stiffness in his joints, he had a constant feeling of chill, and his face, which was normally so lively and expressive, was becoming mask-like and rigid. Princess Mariposa was worried to distraction, for he no longer looked nearly so handsome next to her.

'Can't you do something to cure him?' she demanded of the Royal Physician.

The physician tapped the boy's chest, and looked at his tongue, and felt his pulse. It was like no disease he had ever seen. If he hadn't known the prince was a little boy, he'd have said he was seizing up like a rusty clock, but he could hardly say that to Princess Mariposa.

'Nothing to worry about,' he said. 'It's a condition known as

> That's a typical doctor's answer. He makes up a medical-sounding name (all <u>oxidosis</u> means is <u>rusty disease</u>) and prescribes some medicine that at least won't do any harm. That's one of the first things they teach them in medical school – or it used to be. But the royal physician had a very good bedside manner, and even if he didn't always know how to cure his patients, he soothed and flattered them beautifully.

inflammatory oxidosis. Give him two spoonfuls of cod-liver oil three times a day, and rub his chest with oil of lavender.'

The only one to suspect the truth was his father, and so Prince Otto set off once again for the mines of Schatzberg, and knocked at the door of Dr Kalmenius's workshop.

'Well?' said the clockwork-maker.

'Prince Florian is ill,' said Prince Otto. 'What can we do?'

He described the symptoms, and Dr Kalmenius shrugged his shoulders.

'It's in the nature of clockwork to run down,' was the answer. 'His mainspring was bound to weaken, his escapement to become clogged with dust. I can tell you what will happen next: his skin will stiffen and crack, and split from top to bottom to reveal nothing but dead, seized-up metal inside him. He will never work again.'

'But why didn't you tell me this would happen?'

'You were in such a hurry that you didn't ask.'

'Can't you just wind him up?'

'Impossible.'

'But what can we do?' said Prince Otto in his rage and despair. 'Is there nothing that can save his life? I must have an heir! The survival of the Royal Family depends on it!'

'There is one thing,' said Dr Kalmenius. 'He is failing because he has no heart. Find him a heart, and he will live. But I don't know where you'll find a heart in good condition that its owner is willing to part with. Besides—'

But Prince Otto had left already. He didn't stop to hear the rest of what Dr Kalmenius was going to say. That's often the way with princes; they want instant solutions, not difficult ones that take time and care to bring about. What the great clockwork-maker had been going to say was this: 'The heart that is given must also be kept.' But quite possibly Prince Otto wouldn't have understood anyway.

He rode back to the palace, turning the problem over in his mind. And what a dilemma!

To save his son, he had to sacrifice another human being! What could he do? And whom could he ask to make such a great sacrifice?

And then he thought of the Baron Stelgratz.

Of course! There was no-one better. Baron Stelgratz was an old, trusted adviser, a staunch friend, faithful, brave, and true. The little prince loved him, and he and the baron used to play for hours at mock-battles with Prince Florian's toy soldiers, and the good old nobleman would teach him how to handle a sword or fire a pistol, and tell him all about the animals of the forest.

The more Prince Otto thought about it, the better a choice it seemed. Baron Stelgratz would leap at the chance to give his heart for the family. Better not tell him yet, though; better wait till they were at Dr Kalmenius's workshop; then he would see the necessity quite clearly.

When Prince Otto arrived back at the palace, he found that the little prince had got worse. He could hardly walk without falling over stiffly, and his voice, which had been so full of life and laughter, was becoming more and more like a musical-box; he said very little, but he sang the same few songs over and over. It was clear that he wouldn't last very long.

So Prince Otto went straight to the princess, and persuaded her that a few days' hunting, some brisk exercise in the forest, would do the little child a power of good. Furthermore, he said, Baron Stelgratz would come too; no harm would come to Florian in the baron's company.

So Prince Otto wrapped the little boy up well, and set him in the sledge with Baron Stelgratz beside him, and off they set.

But on the way through the forest, as darkness was falling, the sledge was attacked by wolves.

Maddened by hunger, the great grey beasts poured out of the trees and sprang up at the horses. Prince Otto lashed his whip furiously, and the sledge leapt forward, with the wolves tearing after. Prince Florian sat beside the baron, gripping

The only thing to do when you're chased by wolves is to throw them something tasty, and hope you get away while they eat it. Baron Stelgratz knows this. He's just firing his last bullet. He knows that too.

the side of the sledge, and watched fearfully as the wolf-pack raced closer and closer. Baron Stelgratz emptied his rifle at the pack of leaping, slavering beasts, without deterring them in the least, and the sledge bumped and swayed from side to side on the rough track. At any moment they might crash, and then they would all perish.

'Highness!' cried the baron. 'There is only one thing to do, and I do it with all my heart!'

And the good old man threw himself off the sledge. To save his friends, he sacrificed himself.

Instantly the wild wolves turned on him and tore him to pieces, and the sledge drove on into the silent forest, leaving the snarling, howling beasts far behind.

And *now* what could Prince Otto do?

Drive on, was the only answer; drive on! And hope to find some lonely huntsman or woodcutter, and compensate their family later on. But not a single human being came into view. Behind Prince Otto, the little child, wrapped in furs, was huddled alone on the bouncing seat of the sledge, stiffening, growing colder, changing back into a machine minute by minute. Occasionally the movement of the sledge would shake a little song out of him, but he spoke no more.

Finally they arrived at the mines of Schatzberg, and the house of the clockwork-maker.

And there was only one solution. Prince Otto realized that he had to sacrifice himself, and he was ready. The dynasty was more important than anything else: more important than happiness, than love, than truth, than peace, than honour; far more important than his own life. Prince Otto would give up his heart, cold, fanatical, and proud as it was, for the sake of the future glory of the Royal House.

'You're quite sure this is what you want?' said Dr Kalmenius.

'Don't argue with me! Take out my heart, and put it in my child's breast! It doesn't matter if I die, as long as the dynasty lives!'

The problem now was not the heart, it was the return: how could the child drive back on his own? So, for an extra payment, Dr Kalmenius agreed to animate the dead body of Prince Otto with a small degree of purpose just enough to drive the sledge back to the palace.

The operation was performed. Prince Otto's heart was detached from his breast with subtle instruments, and transferred into the weak and failing body of the silver boy. Instantly, a bright flush of health took the place of Prince Florian's metallic pallor, his eyes opened, and a lively vigour spread through all his limbs. He was alive.

Meanwhile, Dr Kalmenius prepared a simple piece of clockwork apparatus to put in the breast of Prince Otto. It was very crude; when it was wound up, it would make his body drive to the palace. That was all it would do. But it would do it for a long, long time. If Prince Otto's body had been taken to the other side of the world, he would have set off at once for home, though the flesh rotted and fell off his bones, and would never stop until many years later, when his skeleton drove the sledge into the courtyard, with the clockwork ticking in his ribs.

So Dr Kalmenius placed the sleeping body of Prince Florian in the sledge, well wrapped up against the cold, and put the whip into the hand of his dead father, who began at once to lash and lash and lash; and the horses, foaming with terror, began their mad gallop homewards.

And a strange homecoming they had of it. You might have heard the tale of how the sledge drove in at the palace gates, and how the Royal Physician found the clockwork heart. The servants whispered about the dead man whose arm wouldn't keep still, and rumours and guesses flew through the palace and the city like shuttles in a loom, weaving a story of corpses and ghosts, of curses and devils, of death and life and clockwork. But no-one knew the truth.

So time passed. They searched for the baron, they mourned for Prince Otto, Princess Mariposa wept very fetchingly in her widow's black, and Prince Florian grew. Five more years went by, and everyone said how handsome the little prince was, how merry and good, how lucky they were to have such a child as the heir of the family!

But as the winter of the prince's tenth year set in, the dreaded symptoms returned. Prince Florian complained of pains in his joints, of a stiffness in his arms and legs, of a constant chill; and his voice lost its human expressiveness and took on the tinkling sound of a musical-box.

Just as before, the Royal Physician was baffled. 'He has inherited this disease from his father,' he said. 'There can be no question about that.'

'But what disease is it?' said Princess Mariposa.

'A congenital weakness of the heart,' said the physician, sounding as if he knew. 'Combined with inflammatory oxidosis. But if you remember,

Your Highness, we cured that last time by means of healthy exercise in the forest. What Prince Florian needs is a week at the hunting lodge.'

'But last time he went with his father and Baron Stelgratz, and you know what happened then!'

'Ah, medical science has advanced wonderfully in the past five years,' said the physician. 'Have no fear, Your Highness. We shall arrange a hunting trip for the little prince, and he will come back glowing with health, just as he did before.'

But it seemed that the courtiers had less faith in the advance of medical science than the physician, for they all remembered what had happened last time, and none of them wanted to risk a journey through the forest, even if it was to save Prince Florian. This one had gout, that one had an urgent appointment in Venice, another had to visit his aged grandmother in Berlin, and so on, and so on. There was no question of the physician himself going; he was needed every moment at the palace, in case of an emergency. And Princess Mariposa could not possibly go, because the winter air was so bad for her complexion.

Finally, because there was no-one else to do it, they called up one of the grooms and offered him ten silver pieces to take little Prince Florian to the hunting lodge.

'In advance?' the man said, because he had heard the story of what had happened before, and wanted to be sure of his money if anything went wrong.

So they gave him the silver in advance, and the groom tucked Prince Florian into the sledge and harnessed the horses. Princess Mariposa waved from the window as they drove away.

When they had gone some way into the forest, the groom thought: I don't think this kid can last another day; he looks pretty bad to me. And if I go back and tell them he's died, they're bound to punish me. On the other hand, with ten silver pieces and this sledge I can make my way over the border and set up in business on my own account. Buy a little inn, maybe find a wife and have some children of my own. Yes, that's what I'll do. There's nothing that can save this little fellow; I'm doing him a kindness, really; it's a mercy, that's what it is.

So he stopped the sledge at a crossroads and put Prince Florian out.

'Go on,' the groom said, 'go on, you're on your own now, I can't look after you any more. Have a good brisk walk. Stretch your legs. Off you go.'

And he drove away.

Prince Florian obediently started to walk. His legs were very stiff, and the snow lay thickly on the road, but he kept going till he turned a bend and looked down at a little town silent under the moon, where a bell in a church tower was chiming midnight.

A light was glowing in the window of an inn, and an old black cat watched from the shadows.

Prince Florian struggled up to the door and opened it. Being unable to speak, he politely began to sing his one remaining song.

PART THREE

SIR IRONSOUL stopped at once, with a whirr and a click. His sword was inches from Gretl's throat. The prince's song rang out sweetly through the parlour.

Gretl could only stare: in horror at Sir Ironsoul and his sword, in wonder at the prince.

'Where did you come from?' she said. 'Are you the little prince in the story? I think you must be. But how cold you are! And who is this? How sharp his sword is! I don't like him at all. Oh, what must

I do? I feel I'm supposed to do something, but I don't know what it is!'

There was no-one to help. She was alone with the two little figures, one all malice, the other all sweetness. Gretl touched the prince's cheek gently, and found it cold, but her touch awoke something in his machinery for an instant, and he turned his eyes to hers and smiled.

'Oh, you poor thing!' she cried.

He opened his lips, and sang one or two notes.

'I know what it is,' said Gretl. 'You're not well. And I don't like that little knight one bit, and I don't want to leave you here with him, but I know whose fault this is. It was Fritz who made the story up. If only we could find out how it finished . . .'

She looked at the stove, where Fritz had thrown the sheets of paper on which his story was written. She had thought they were all destroyed, but crumpled up on the floor, in the shadow, there was one piece left unburnt.

She picked it up and straightened it out. It was the very page he had been reading when the stranger had come in. On it were the words:

*He was very tall and thin, with a prominent
nose and jaw. His eyes blazed like coals in
caverns of darkness. His hair was long and grey,
and he wore a black cloak with a loose hood like
that of a monk; he had a harsh grating voice
and his expression was full of savage curiosity.
And that was the man who —*

There was no more. The story stopped at that point.

'That was exactly when he came in!' said Gretl to herself. But there were another few words scribbled below, and, peering closely, she managed to make them out.

*Oh, this is impossible! How can I write
an ending to this story? I'll have to make it*

up when I get there, and hope I do it well.
If I come up with something good, the
devil can have my soul!

Gretl's eyes widened, and she bit her lip in horror. People shouldn't say things like that! 'Well,' she said to herself, 'he started it all off, and I'm going to make him finish it. You sit in here and keep warm, Prince Florian, if that's who you really are, and I'll go and fetch Fritz. He's the only one who can sort it out.'

So she threw on her cloak, and set off to the house where Fritz the storyteller had his lodging.

Meanwhile, Karl had been preparing the place in the mechanism of the great clock that was set aside for his masterpiece. Feverish with excitement, he hurried down the staircase of the clock tower and across the square to the inn. The old cat Putzi was still outside, sitting on the window sill, watching everything as he licked his paws and cleaned his ears. It was cold out there, and he was wondering about coming in for a snooze by the stove.

But Karl didn't notice him. He had other things than cats on his mind. He went in quietly and shut the door, and then he stopped in alarm, for there was the canvas, thrown aside, and there was Sir Ironsoul, sword upraised, on the other side of the room.

Karl's heart missed a beat. Had someone else come in and disturbed the little knight? There was no-one dead, at least, but why had the figure moved? Karl looked around, and then he saw the little prince sitting politely in his chair, watching him. A thousand strange fears ran over his skin.

Karl opened his mouth to speak, and then realized that the child wasn't alive after all. It was another clockwork figure like Sir Ironsoul! And a far finer one, by the look of it. He peered at it closely. The hair, the finest gold wires he had ever seen; the bloom on the silver cheeks, like a butterfly's wing; the eyes, bright blue jewels, almost alive in the way they seemed to look at him!

Only Dr Kalmenius could have created this. And he must have brought it for Karl. What did the figure do?

Karl reached out and lifted the prince's hand from his lap. With a little flicker of his energy, Prince Florian shook Karl's hand, and sang a bar of music for him. Karl's hair stood on end, for an idea had just come to him. Why not put *this* figure in the clock instead of Sir Ironsoul? It was more finely finished, and a handsome little boy who sang a pretty tune would be far more popular with the crowds than a faceless knight who did nothing but threaten people with a sword.

And then he could keep Sir Ironsoul for himself.

And then ... Oh, how his mind raced. He could travel the world. He could become famous giving exhibitions and demonstrations.

He became quite dizzy as he thought of the uses to which he could put the metal knight. The gold he could steal, the forbidden treasures that could be his, if he had a secret accomplice, like Sir Ironsoul, who could be relied on always to kill and never to give him away! All he would have to do would be to trick his intended victim into saying the word 'devil', and leave Sir Ironsoul nearby to play his part. He, Karl, could be somewhere else entirely, playing cards with a dozen witnesses, or even in church surrounded by the faithful. No-one would ever know!

So excited did he become that he lost all sense of what was right. The church, his father and mother and brother and sister, Herr Ringelmann, every influence for good he'd ever known was whirled away into the darkness, and all he could see was the wealth and power that would be his if he used Sir Ironsoul in that way.

And before he could change his mind, he threw the canvas over the knight, tucked the stiffening figure of Prince Florian under his arm, and set off back to the clock tower.

Meanwhile, Gretl was struggling through the snow towards the house where Fritz lodged. She could see from the end of the street that all the windows were dark except one in the attic where Fritz often used to work throughout the night. She had to knock half a dozen times before the landlady came grumbling to open the door.

'Who is it? What do you want at this time of night? Oh, it's you, child; what in the world are you after?'

'I've got to speak to Herr Fritz! It's very important!'

Mumbling and frowning, the old lady stepped aside and said, 'Yes, I heard all about that business at the inn. Making up wicked stories! Frightening people! I'll be glad when he's gone. In fact I've got half a mind to give him notice. Go on up, child, top of the stairs and keep going. No, you can't have a candle, this is the only one I've got and I need it myself. You've got sharp eyes; make do.'

So Gretl climbed the four staircases to the top of the house, each one darker and narrower than the one below, and came at last to a tiny landing where a line of light glowed beneath a door. There she knocked, and a nervous voice answered:

'Who is it? What do you want?'

'It's Gretl, Herr Fritz! From the inn! I've got to speak to you!'

'Come in, then – as long as you're by yourself . . .'

Gretl opened the door. She found Fritz standing in the light of a smoky lamp, throwing paper after paper into a leather bag which was bulging with his clothes and books and other bits and pieces. A glass of plum brandy stood on the table beside him. He had already drunk quite a lot, by the look of him, for his eyes were wild, his cheeks were flushed, and his hair was standing on end.

'What is it?' he said. 'What do you want?'

'That story you told us,' Gretl began, but she got no further, for the young man put his hands over his ears and shook his head violently.

'Don't speak of it! I wish I'd never begun it! I wish I'd never told a story in my life!'

'But you've got to listen to me!' she said. 'Something dreadful's going to happen, and I don't know what it is because you didn't finish writing the story!'

'How do you know I didn't finish it?' he said.

She showed him the sheet of paper she'd found. He groaned, and put his face in his hands.

'Groaning won't help,' she said. 'You've got to finish the story properly. What happens next?'

'I don't know!' he cried. 'I dreamed the first part of it, and it was so strange and horrible that I couldn't resist writing it down and pretending it was mine . . . But I couldn't think of any more!'

'But what were you going to do when you got to that part?' she said.

'Make it up, of course!' he said. 'I've done that before. I often do it. I enjoy the risk, you see. I start telling a story with no idea what's going to happen at the end, and I make it up when I get there. Sometimes it's even better than writing it down first. I was sure I could do it with this one. But when the door opened and the old man came in, I must have panicked . . . Oh, I wish I'd never begun! I'll never tell a story again!'

'You must tell the end of this one, though,' said Gretl, 'or something bad will happen. You've got to.'

'I can't!'

'You must.'

'I couldn't!'

'You *have* to.'

'Impossible,' he said. 'I can't control it any more. I wound it up and set it going, and it'll just have to work itself out. I wash my hands of it. I'm off!'

This is Fritz: useless, you see. Quite irresponsible. But then Fritz was only playing at being a storyteller. If he was a proper craftsman like a clockwork-maker he'd have known that all actions have their consequences. For every tick there is a tock. For every once upon a time there must be a story to follow, because if a story doesn't, something else will, and it might not be as harmless as a story.

'But you can't! Where are you going?'

'Anywhere! Berlin, Vienna, Prague – as far away as I can get!'

And he poured himself another glass of plum brandy and swallowed it all in one go.

So Gretl sighed and turned to leave.

At the same time as she was feeling her way down the dark stairs in Fritz's lodging-house, Karl was going back into the inn. He had taken little Florian up to the clock tower and fastened him to the frame, ignoring the prince's helpless struggles and his musical requests for mercy. When morning came, there he would be, Karl's masterpiece, on show as everyone expected. And Karl would receive everyone's congratulations, and his certificate of competence from Herr Ringelmann, and he'd be entered in the roll of master clockwork-makers; and then he could leave the town and make his way with Sir Ironsoul into the wide world, where power and fortune awaited him!

But when he opened the door of the inn to collect the little knight and hide him in his lodgings, he felt a shiver of fear. He stood on the threshold, afraid and unwilling to enter. And once again he took no notice of Putzi the cat, who jumped down from the windowsill when he saw the door open. There's no need to be superstitious about cats, but they are our fellow creatures, and we shouldn't ignore them. It would have been polite of Karl to offer his knuckles for the old cat to rub his head against, but Karl was wound up too tightly for politeness.

So he didn't see the cat stalking in past his legs.

Finally Karl gathered his courage and went in. How still the room was! And how sinister that

Trouble will come of this, you mark my words. It always pays to be polite, even to dumb creatures.

little figure under the canvas! And that sword-point: how wickedly sharp! Sharp enough to have pierced the canvas already, and be glinting in the lamplight . . .

Some coals settled in the stove, sending a little flare of red out on the floor, and making Karl jump nervously. The glow made him think of the fires of hell, and he sweated and mopped his brow.

Then the long-case clock in the corner began to whirr and wheeze, preparing to strike. Karl leapt as if he'd been discovered in the act of murder, and then leant weakly against the table, his heart beating like thunder.

'Oh, I can't bear this!' he said. 'I've done nothing wrong, have I? Then why am I so nervous? What is there to be frightened of?'

Hearing his words, old Putzi decided that here was someone who might give him a little milk, if he asked nicely; so the cat jumped up on the table beside him, and rubbed himself on Karl's arm.

Feeling this, Karl turned in shock to see a black cat who had appeared, as it seemed, out of nowhere. Naturally, this was too much for Karl. He leapt away from the table with an exclamation of horror.

Here it is. Here comes the trouble.

'Oh! What the devil—?'

And then he clapped his hands to his mouth, as if trying to cram the word back inside. But it was too late. In the corner of the room, the metal figure had begun to move. The canvas fell to the floor, and Sir Ironsoul raised his sword even higher, and turned his helmet this way and that until he saw where Karl was cowering.

There's no way of avoiding this. I'd save the wretch if I could, but the story is wound up, and it must all come out. And I'm afraid Karl deserved a bad end. He was lazy and bad-tempered, but worse than that, he had a wicked heart. He really would have used Sir Ironsoul to kill people and make money in the way he'd thought about. So close your eyes and think of something else for a moment; Karl is ticking his final tock.

'No! No! Stop – wait – the tune – let me whistle the tune—'

But his lips were too dry. Frantic, he licked them with a dry tongue. No use! He couldn't produce a sound. Nearer and nearer came the little knight with the sharp sword, and Karl stumbled away, trying to hum, to sing, to whistle, and all he could do was cry and stammer and sob, and the knight came closer and closer.

When Gretl got back to the inn she heard Putzi miaowing inside, and said as she opened the door, 'How did you get in, you silly cat?'

Putzi shot out into the square as Gretl came in, and wouldn't stop to be petted. She shut the door and looked around for the prince, but she didn't see him anywhere. Instead, a horrid sight met her eyes, and made her shiver and clutch her breast. There in the middle of the room stood Sir Ironsoul, with his helmet shining blankly and his

Time is running out, like sand in the hourglass, which is another kind of clock, after all. Will Gretl get to the prince in time? She's in time now: she's right inside the clock, at the very heart of time. She'll get there.

sword slanting down. He was holding it like that because the point was in the throat of Karl the apprentice, who lay stark dead beside him.

Gretl nearly fainted, but she was a brave girl, and she had seen what lay in Karl's hand. It was the heavy iron key of the clock tower. With her mind in a whirl, she was still able to guess part of what had happened, if not all of it, and she realized what Karl must have done with the prince. She took the key from his hand and ran out of the inn and across the square to the great dark tower.

She turned the key in the lock and began to climb for the second time that night, but these stairs were higher and steeper than those in Fritz's lodging. And they were darker, too; and there were bats that flitted through the air; and the wind groaned across the mouths of the mighty bells, and made their ropes swing dismally.

But up and up she climbed, until she came to the lowest of the clock-chambers, where the oldest and simplest part of the mechanism was housed.

In the darkness she felt her way around the huge iron cog-wheels, the thick ropes, the stiff metal figures of St Wolfgang and the devil, but she didn't find the prince; and so she climbed on. She ran her hands over the Archangel Michael, and in his armour he reminded her of Sir Ironsoul, and she took her hands away quickly. She felt up the side of a figure in a painted robe, and her fingers explored his face until she realized that it was the skull-face of Death, and she took her hands away from him, too.

The higher she climbed, the more noise the clock made: a ticking and a tocking, a clicking and a creaking, a whirring and a rumbling. She clambered over struts and levers and chains and cogwheels, and the further she went, the more she felt as if she, too, were becoming part of the clock; and all the time, she peered into the dark and felt around and listened with all her might.

Finally she clambered up through a trapdoor into the very topmost chamber, and found silver moonlight shining in on such a complexity of mechanical parts that she could make no sense of them at all. At the same moment, she heard a little song. It was the prince calling to her.

Dazzled by the moonlight, Gretl blinked and rubbed her eyes. And there was Prince Florian, with the very last of his clockwork life, singing like a nightingale.

'Oh! You poor cold thing! He's fastened you so tightly I can't undo the bolts – oh, that was wicked! He was going to leave you here and run away, I'm sure. What's the matter with you, Prince Florian? I'm sure you'd tell me if you could. I think you're ill, that's what the trouble is. I think you need warming up. You're too cold, but that's hardly surprising, seeing what they've done with you. Never mind! If I can't get you down, I'll stay up here with you. I can wrap my cloak around us both, you'll see. We're better off up here in any case, if you ask me. The things that have been going on! You'd never believe it!

I won't tell you now, because you wouldn't go to sleep. I'll tell you in the morning, I promise. Are you comfortable, Prince Florian? You don't have to speak if you don't want to; you can just nod.'

Prince Florian nodded, and Gretl tucked her cloak around them, and held the little boy in her arms as she went to sleep. The last thing she thought was: He *is* getting warmer, I'm sure; I can feel it!

The morning came. All through the town, visitors and townsfolk alike were getting dressed and eating their breakfasts hungrily, eager to see the new figure in the famous clock.

The snow-laden rooftops glittered and gleamed in the bright blue air, and the fragrance of roasting coffee and fresh-baked rolls drifted through the streets. And as time drew on towards ten o'clock, a strange rumour went round the town: the clockmaker's apprentice had been found dead! Murdered, what was more!

The police called Herr Ringelmann in to look at the body. The old clockmaker was shocked and dismayed to see his apprentice lying dead.

'The poor boy! It was his day of fame! Whatever can have happened? What a disaster! Who can have done this terrible thing?'

'Do you recognize this figure, Herr Ringelmann?' said the sergeant. 'This clockwork knight?'

'No, I've never seen it before in my life. Is that Karl's blood on its sword?'

'I'm afraid so. Do you think he could have made this figure?'

'No, certainly not! The figure he made is up in the clock. That's the tradition, you know, sergeant: he was going to fit his new figure in the clock on the last evening of his apprenticeship, just as I did in my time. Karl was a good boy; a little quiet and morose, perhaps, but a good apprentice; I'm sure he did what he was supposed to do, and we'll see his new figure when it comes out in a minute or so. What a sad occasion, instead of a happy one! The new figure will have to be his memorial, poor boy.'

Nothing was right that morning. The innkeeper was desperately anxious, because Gretl was missing. What could have happened to her? The whole town was in a ferment. A crowd had gathered outside the inn, and they watched the policemen carrying out Karl's body on a stretcher, covered by a piece of canvas. But they didn't look that way for long, because it was nearly ten o'clock, and the time had come for the mechanism to reveal the new figure.

All eyes turned upwards. There was even more interest than usual, because of the strange circumstances of Karl's death, and the square was so crowded that you couldn't see the cobbles; people were crammed shoulder to shoulder, and every face was turned up like a flower to the sun.

The hour began to strike. The ancient clock wheezed and whirred as the mechanism came into play. The familiar figures came out first, and bowed or gestured or simply twirled on their toes; there was St Wolfgang, throwing the devil over his shoulder; there was the Archangel Michael with his glittering armour; there was the figure Herr Ringelmann had made for the end of *his* apprenticeship, many years ago: a little boy who popped out, thumbed his nose at Death, and twiddled his fingers before ducking out of sight again.

And then came the new figure.

But it wasn't one figure, it was two: two sleeping children, a girl and a boy, so lifelike and beautiful that they didn't seem to be made of clockwork at all.

A gasp of surprise went up from the crowd as the two little figures yawned and stretched and looked down, clutching each other for fear of the height, and yet laughing and chatting together in the bright morning light, and pointing out the sights around the square.

'A masterpiece!' cried someone, and another voice said, 'The best figures ever made!'

And more voices joined in:

'A work of genius!'

'Incomparable!'

'So lifelike – look at the way they're waving at us!'

'I've never seen anything like it!'

But Herr Ringelmann had his suspicions, and peered upwards, shading his eyes. And then the innkeeper, looking up with everyone else, saw who it was, and gave a cry of joy.

'It's my Gretl! She's safe! Gretl, keep still! We'll come up and bring you down safely! Don't move! We'll be there in a moment!'

And very soon, the two children were safely on the ground. Two children, because the prince wasn't clockwork any more; he was a child as real as any other, and so he remained. 'The heart that is given must also be kept,' as Dr Kalmenius had been about to say to Prince Otto; but the prince

Out of the night, and out of the past. Gretl has made Florian a present of her heart, and what they're looking at is the future.

didn't listen, did he? No-one could guess where the little boy had come from, and Florian couldn't remember. Presently everyone accepted that he had been lost, and that they had better look after him; so they did.

As for the metal knight with the bloodstained sword, Herr Ringelmann took it away to his workshop to examine closely. When they asked him about it later, he could only shake his head.

'I don't know how anyone expected that to work,' he said. 'It's full of miscellaneous bits and pieces, and they're not even connected up properly: broken springs, wheels with cogs missing, rusty gears – worthless rubbish, all of it! I do hope Karl didn't make it; I thought better of him than that. Well, my friends, it's just a mystery, and I don't suppose we'll ever get to the bottom of it.'

Nor did they, because the one person who might have been able to tell them the truth was Fritz, and he had been so badly scared that he'd left town before the sun rose, and he never came back. He fled to another part of Germany, and he was going to stop writing fiction altogether, until he found he could earn lots of money by making up speeches for politicians. As for what happened to Dr Kalmenius, who can say? He was only a character in a story, after all.

And if Gretl knew more than anyone, she said nothing about it. She had lost her heart to the prince, and kept it too, which was how he came to be turned from clockwork into boy. So they both lived happily ever after; and that was how they all wound up.

Read on for a preview of

THE SCARECROW
AND HIS SERVANT

LIGHTNING

ONE DAY old Mr Pandolfo, who hadn't been feeling at all well, decided that it was time to make a scarecrow. The birds had been very troublesome. Come to that, his rheumatism had been troublesome, and the soldiers had been troublesome, and the weather had been troublesome, and his cousins had been troublesome. It was all getting a bit too much for him. Even his old pet raven had flown away.

He couldn't do anything about his rheumatism, or the soldiers, or the weather, or his cousins, who were the biggest problem of all. There was a whole family of them, the Buffalonis, and they wanted to get hold of his land and divert all the springs and streams, and drain all the wells, and put up a factory to make weedkiller and rat poison and insecticide.

All those troubles were too big for old Mr Pandolfo to manage, but he thought he could do something about the birds, at least. So he put together a fine-looking scarecrow, with a big solid turnip for a head and a sturdy broomstick for a backbone, and dressed him in an old tweed suit, and stuffed him tightly with straw. Then he tucked a short letter inside him, wrapped in oilskin for safety.

'There you are,' he said. 'Now you remember what your job is, and remember where you belong. Be courteous, and be brave, and be honourable, and be kind. And the best of blooming luck.'

He stuck the scarecrow in the middle of the wheatfield, and went home to lie down, because he wasn't feeling well at all.

That night another farmer came along and stole the scarecrow, being too lazy to make one himself. And the next night someone else came along and stole him again.

So little by little the scarecrow moved away from the place where he was made, and he got more and more tattered and torn, and finally he didn't look nearly as smart as he'd done when Mr Pandolfo put him together. He stood in the middle of a muddy field, and he stayed there.

But one night there was a thunderstorm. It was a very violent one, and everyone in the district shivered and trembled and jumped as the thunder went off like cannon-fire and the lightning lashed down like whips. The scarecrow stood there in the wind and the rain, taking no notice.

And so he might have stayed; but then there came one of those million-to-one chances that are like winning the lottery. All his molecules and atoms and elementary particles and whatnot were lined up in exactly the right way to switch on when the lightning struck him, which it did at two in the morning, fizzing its way through his turnip and down his broomstick and into the mud.

The Scarecrow blinked with surprise and looked all around. There wasn't much to see except a field of mud, and not much light to see it by except the flashes of lightning.

Still, there wasn't a bird in sight.

'Excellent,' said the Scarecrow.

On the same night, a small boy called Jack happened to be sheltering in a barn not far away. The thunder was so loud that it woke him out of his sleep with a jump. At first he thought it was cannon-fire, and he sat up terrified with his eyes wide open. He could think of nothing worse than soldiers and guns; if it weren't for the soldiers, he'd still have a family and a home and a bed to sleep in.

But as he sat there with his heart thumping, he heard the downpour of the rain on the roof, and realized that the bang had only been thunder and not gunfire. He gave a sigh of relief and lay down again, shivering and sneezing and turning over and over in the hay trying to get warm, until finally he fell asleep.

By the morning the storm had cleared away, and the sky was a bright cold blue. Jack woke up again feeling colder than ever, and hungry too. But he knew how to look for food, and before long he'd gathered up some grains of wheat and a couple of turnip tops and a limp carrot, and he sat in the doorway of the barn in the sunlight to eat them.

'Could be worse,' he said to himself.

He ate very slowly to make it last, and then he just sat there, getting warm. Someone would come along soon to chase him away, but for the moment he was safe.

Then he heard a voice calling from across the fields. Jack was curious, so he stood up and shaded his eyes to look. The shouting came from somewhere in the field beyond the road, and since he had nothing else to do, Jack stood up and walked along towards it.

The shouts came from a scarecrow, in the middle of the muddiest field in sight, and he was waving his arms wildly and yelling at the top of his voice and leaning over at a crazy angle.

'Help!' he was shouting. 'Come and help me!'

'I think I'm going mad,' said Jack to himself. 'Still, look at that poor old thing – I'll go and help him anyway. He looks madder than I feel.'

So he stepped on to the muddy field, and struggled out to the middle, where the Scarecrow was waiting.

To tell the truth, Jack felt a little nervous, because it isn't every day you find a Scarecrow talking to you.

'Now, tell me, young man,' said the Scarecrow, as soon as Jack was close enough to hear, 'are there any birds around? Any crows, for example? I can't see behind me. Are they hiding?'

His voice was rich and sonorous. His head was made of a great knobbly turnip, with a broad crack for a mouth and a long thin sprout for a nose and two bright little stones for eyes. He had a tattered straw hat, now badly singed, and a soggy woollen scarf, and an old tweed jacket full of holes, and his rake-handle arms had gloves stuffed with straw on the ends of them, one glove leather and the other wool. He also had a pair of threadbare trousers, but since he only had one leg, the empty trouser leg trailed down beside him. Everything was the colour of mud. Jack scratched his head and looked all around.

'No,' he said, 'no crows anywhere. No birds at all.'

'That's a good job done,' said the Scarecrow. 'Now I want to move on, but I need another leg. If you go and find me a leg, I shall be very obliged. Just like this one, only the opposite,' he added, and he lifted his trouser leg daintily to show a stout stick set firmly in the earth.

'All right,' said Jack. 'I can do that.'

So he set off towards the wood at the edge of the field, and clambered through the undergrowth looking for the right sort of stick. He found one before long, and took it back to the Scarecrow.

'Let me see,' said the Scarecrow. 'Hold it up beside me. That's it. Now slide it up inside the leg of my trousers.'

The end of the stick was broken and splintered and it wasn't easy to push it up the soggy, muddy trouser leg, but Jack finally got it all the way up, and then he jumped, because he felt it twitch in his hand.

He let go, and the new leg swung itself down beside the other. But as soon as the Scarecrow tried to move, the new foot became stuck just like the first one. The harder he struggled, the deeper he sank.

Finally he stopped, and looked at Jack. It was astonishing how much expression he could manage with his gash-mouth and stone-eyes.

'Young man,' he said, 'I have a proposition to make. Here you are, an honest and willing youth, and here am I, a Scarecrow of enterprise and talent. What would you say if I offered you the position of my personal servant?'

'What would my duties be?' said Jack.

'To accompany me throughout the world, to fetch and carry, to wash, cook, and attend to my needs. In return, I have nothing to offer but excitement and glory. We might sometimes go hungry, but we shall never want for adventure. Well, my boy? What do you say?'

'I'll do it,' said Jack. 'I've got nothing else to do except starve, and nowhere to live except ditches and empty barns. So I might as well have a job, and thank you, Mr Scarecrow, I'll take it.'

The Scarecrow extended his hand, and Jack shook it warmly.

'Your first job is to get me out of this mud,' said the Scarecrow.

So Jack heaved the Scarecrow's two legs out of the mud and carried him to the road. He hardly weighed anything at all.

'Which way shall we go?' said Jack.

They looked both ways. In one direction there was a forest, and in the other there was a line of hills. There was no-one in sight.

'That way!' said the Scarecrow, pointing to the hills.

So they set off, with the sun on their backs, and the green hills ahead.

In a farmhouse not far behind them, a lawyer was explaining something to a farmer.

'My name is Cercorelli,' he said, 'and I specialize in finding things for my employers, the distinguished and highly respectful Buffaloni Corporation, of Bella Fontana.'

The farmer gasped. He was a stout, red-faced, idle character, and he was afraid of this lean and silky lawyer, who was dressed entirely in black.

'Oh! The Buffalonis! Yes, indeed, Mr Cercorelli,' he said. 'What can I do to help? Anything! Just name it!'

'It's a small matter,' said the lawyer, 'but one of sentimental importance to my clients. It concerns a scarecrow. It was made by a distant cousin of the Chairman of the Corporation, and it seems to have vanished from its place of origin. My client Mr Giovanni Buffaloni is a very warm-hearted and family-minded man, and he would like to restore the scarecrow to its original home, in memory of his dear cousin who made it.'

The lawyer looked through some papers, and the farmer ran his finger around the inside of his shirt collar, and gulped.

'Well, I, um . . .' he said faintly.

'One might almost think that scarecrows had the power of movement!' said Mr Cercorelli, smiling in a sinister way. 'This fellow has been wandering. I've traced him through several farms already, and now I discover that he made his way to yours.'

'I – er – I think I know the scarecrow you mention,' said the farmer. 'I nick – I bought him from someone else, who didn't need him no more.'

'Oh, good. May we go and see if he is the right one?'

'Well, of course, I'd do anything for the Buffalonis, important people, wouldn't want to upset them, but . . . Well, he's gone.'

'Gone . . . *again?*' said the lawyer, narrowing his eyes.

'I went out this morning, to – er – to tidy him up a bit, and he wasn't there. Mind you, there was a big storm last night. He might have blown away.'

'Oh, dear. That is very unfortunate. Mr Buffaloni takes a dim view of people who do not look after his property. I think I can say that his degree of disappointment will be considerable.'

The farmer was quaking with alarm.

'If I ever hear anything about the scarecrow,' he said, 'anything at all, I'll report to you at once.'

'I think that would be very wise,' said Mr Cercorelli. 'Here is my card. Now show me the field from which the scarecrow vanished.'

ABOUT THE AUTHOR

PHILIP PULLMAN was born in 1946 in Norwich, Norfolk. He spent a lot of his childhood on board ships, as his father and stepfather were both in the Royal Air Force and his mother and brother seemed to be constantly following them around the world by sea.

Philip read English at Oxford University and for a long time he taught in schools before becoming a full-time writer. He is now one of our best storytellers. He has written many books for children and has won numerous awards for his work.

The Firework-Maker's Daughter was a Gold Medal Smarties prize-winner, *Clockwork* was a Silver Medal Smarties prize-winner, and *Northern Lights*, the first volume in his trilogy, *His Dark Materials*, won the Carnegie Medal and was joint winner of the Guardian Children's Fiction Prize. His novel *The Amber Spyglass* was the first ever children's book to win the overall Whitbread Award. The *His Dark Materials* trilogy has been made into an acclaimed production at the National Theatre. Philip Pullman lives in Oxford, and is married with two sons.

I WAS A RAT!

A fairy tale filled with fun and magic for young and old from the master storyteller and creator of *His Dark Materials*

'*I was a rat!*' Roger insists, and insists . . . In fact, when Bob the cobbler and his washerwoman wife, Joan, find the young boy abandoned on their doorstep, these are the only words he says. And he does have ratty behaviour, it's true.

Staying with Bob and Joan, however, Roger learns quickly to behave more like a human child. They try to find his parents, but the orphanage, police and hospital all have nothing on their records about a lost boy in the city. What is the truth? As more and more people find out about Roger the mysterious rat-boy he faces more and more danger. But sometimes help comes from the most unexpected of places . . .

'Fairy tale, satire, slapstick humour and suspenseful melodrama . . . a glorious tale' *Guardian*

'A comic genius of children's fiction' *The Times*

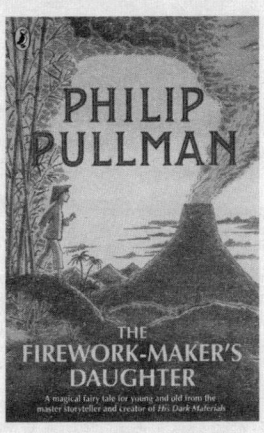

THE FIREWORK-MAKER'S DAUGHTER

**A magical fairy tale for young and old
from the master storyteller and creator
of *His Dark Materials***

Lila doesn't just want to be a Firework-Maker's
daughter, she wants to be a Firework-Maker herself.
But although she's learned a lot she still must get
through the most difficult and dangerous part of her
apprenticeship – and her father won't tell her what it is.

In search of this final Firework-Making secret,
Lila heads off alone on a journey. It is a journey
filled with dangers beyond anything she could have
imagined, a journey on which she will learn so much
more than the one secret she set out to find . . .

'This is a book you will want to read over and
over again' *Sunday Times*

'One of those rare books with a confident magic . . .
sheer genius' *Independent*

COUNT KARLSTEIN

On All Souls' Eve, the Demon Huntsman will ride . . .

All Souls' Eve is a night when nobody in the village of Karlstein dares to leave their homes. For that is the night that Zamiel, the Demon Huntsman, prowls through the forests in search of his prey . . .

This year, however, the Huntsman doesn't need to go searching. He knows exactly where to find his human prey. Ten years ago, he made a deal with the Count of Karlstein – and now the Demon Huntsman has come to collect his prize . . .

Count Karlstein has offered up the lives of his two young nieces, Lucy and Charlotte. Lucky for the orphaned sisters, the Count's maid, Hildi, has heard his evil plan and is determined that they will not be this year's prey – not on her watch . . .

The very first children's novel by Philip Pullman, the creator of *His Dark Materials*, *Count Karlstein* is a deliciously terrifying, wickedly funny adventure.

'A masterly storyteller' *Independent*

SPRING-HEELED JACK

One dark and stormy night it is time for the original superhero to spring into action . . .

Rose and Lily and their little brother Ned live in an orphanage – a terrible place, where the porridge is thin and cold, and nobody smiles. One dark and stormy night they decide enough is enough, and they run away. But hiding in the shadows, as they make their way through the dangerous back streets of London, is Mack the Knife: the most villainous of villains . . .

Hiding above the streets, leaping through the air, is Spring-Heeled Jack. He dresses like the devil and his name creates shivers in people, but he is ready for action against the evil-doers and scallywags of the city's dark streets – Mack the Knife included – and he might just be able to save the orphans.

A fun thriller of an adventure told in words and pictures from master storyteller Philip Pullman.

'A fantastic adventure which will have even reluctant readers hiding under the cover with a torch'
Sunday Express